Dear mouse friends,
Welcome to the world of

Geronimo Stilton

The Editorial Staff of
The Rodent's Gazette

1. Linda Thinslice
2. Sweetie Cheesetriangle
3. Ratella Redfur
4. Soya Mousehao
5. Cheesita de la Pampa
6. Mouseanna Mousetti
7. Yale Youngmouse
8. Toni Tinypaw
9. Tina Spicytail
10. William Shortpaws
11. Valerie Vole
12. Trap Stilton
13. Branwen Musclemouse
14. Zeppola Zap
15. Merenguita Gingermouse
16. Ratsy O'Shea
17. Rodentrick Roundrat
18. Teddy von Muffler
19. Thea Stilton
20. Erronea Misprint
21. Pinky Pick
22. Ya-ya O'Cheddar
23. Mousella MacMouser
24. Kreamy O'Cheddar
25. Blasco Tabasco
26. Toffie Sugarsweet
27. Tylerat Truemouse
28. Larry Keys
29. Michael Mouse
30. Geronimo Stilton
31. Benjamin Stilton
32. Briette Finerat
33. Raclette Finerat

Geronimo Stilton
A learned and brainy
mouse; editor of
The Rodent's Gazette

Thea Stilton
Geronimo's sister and
special correspondent at
The Rodent's Gazette

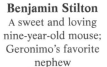

Trap Stilton
An awful joker;
Geronimo's cousin and
owner of the store
Cheap Junk for Less

Benjamin Stilton
A sweet and loving
nine-year-old mouse;
Geronimo's favorite
nephew

Geronimo Stilton

ALL BECAUSE
OF A CUP
OF COFFEE

Scholastic Inc.

New York   Toronto   London   Auckland   Sydney
Mexico City   New Delhi   Hong Kong   Buenos Aires

No part of this publication may be reproduced in whole or in part, or stored in a retrieval system, or transmitted in any form or by any means, electronic, mechanical, photocopying, recording, or otherwise, without written permission of the publisher. For information regarding permission, write to Edizioni Piemme S.p.A., Italy

ISBN-13: 978-0-439-55972-0
ISBN-10: 0-439-55972-3

Original title: *Tutta colpa di un caffè con panna*
Text by Geronimo Stilton
Original cover by Larry Keys
Illustrations by Larry Keys, revised by Topetti & Rattozzi
Special thanks to Kathryn Cristaldi
Cover and interior design by Kay Petronio

26 25 24 23 22   11 12/0

Printed in the U.S.A.   40
First printing, August 2004

All Because of a Cup of Coffee

A cup of coffee? What's a cup of coffee got to do with it?

Everything! But let me explain. See, that morning I was having breakfast at the Tail Trap Diner. They have the best hot cheese buns. But stay away from the Spanish omelet. It's so spicy, it will curl your whiskers! Anyway, I was happily **munching** away when some mouse spilled coffee on me. My jacket was soaked! I was *FUMING!* I whirled around, ready to squeak. Instead, my jaw hit the ground.

A female mouse stood in front of me. No, she wasn't just any mouse. She was the most **BEAUTIFUL MOUSE** in the world! She stared at her **EMPTY** cup. Then she stared at my jacket. "*So sorry*," she whispered in a sweet voice.

I tried to speak but it felt like my tongue was tied in a knot. What do you say to such a stunning rodent? She was so *charming*. She was so *sophisticated*. She could have been on the cover of *Glamour Mouse*!

"Um, my Stilton is name; I mean, my Geronimo is Stilton; I mean, my name is *Geronimo Stilton*!" I stammered.

I tried to shake her paw, but I slipped on the spilled coffee. I **CRASHED** into a table of rats having breakfast. I landed snoutdown in a plate of waffles and whipped cream.

"Do you mind?" sniffed the rats. "This is a business breakfast."

I staggered off. But I couldn't see. I had whipped cream in my eyes. I bumped into another table. This time, two bottles of Tabasco sauce got stuck in my nostrils. "Cheese niblets!" I cried, stumbling away. Next thing I knew, my tail was stuck in a fan. "owWW!" I shrieked. Then I hit a wall. A big, furry wall.

"Watch it, furbrain!" the wall growled. Uh-oh. That wasn't a wall. It was Burt Bruiser Mouse. He was the biggest and meanest rodent on Mouse Island. I tried to run, but I was **FROZEN** with fear.

Suddenly, Burt lifted me up and tossed me out the door. I landed on the trolley tracks. I tried to get up, but my tail was stuck in the rails.

Just then, I heard the train whistle. Rotten rats' teeth! A trolley was headed right for me.

"HELP!" I squeaked at the top of my lungs.

The owner of the Furever Green Garden Center ran toward me. "Don't panic, Mr. Stilton!" he shouted. "I'll save you! I'll just chop your tail off with my hedge clippers!" He waved the sharp scissors in the air. chop-*chop!*

"Paws off my tail!" I shrieked. "I'd rather be run over by a trolley!"

And that's exactly what happened.

My tail was stuck in the rails.

THE RODENT'S GAZETTE

Luckily, I survived. So did my tail. After the trolley hit, I yanked my tail from the rails. Then I stumbled to my paws. I had a huge grin on my face. I felt so **happy**. So **CAREFREE**. So *ALIVE*. Oh, yes, I was happy to be alive. And I was happy for another reason, too. I had fallen in *love!* Getting knocked in the head by that trolley had made me realize something. The beautiful mouse in the diner was the one for me. I just knew she was my soul mouse. Now all I had to do was tell her.

I reached my office in a daze. Oops, I forgot to tell you. I run a daily newspaper. It's called *The Rodent's Gazette.*

As soon as I walked into the editorial

room, my sister, Thea, **ATTACKED** me.

"Geronimooo! Where have you been?" she shrieked. "The meeting has already started!"

I just grinned from ear to ear. "Meeting? What meeting?" I murmured absentmindedly.

My sister stared at me. "What's with the bottles in your nose? And what happened **to your jacket**? You look like you just got run over by a trolley!" she declared.

I smiled. "Yes, it was a trolley. It ran right over me," I giggled. I was still dreaming about the mouse from the diner. "Such gorgeous fur," I mumbled. "And that smile could light up the darkest mouse hole."

My sister stamped her paw. Then she grabbed me by the whiskers. "Hello in there! *Is anybody* **home?!**" she shouted in my ear. "What are you talking about? You are not making any sense. Did you drink too much coffee this morning?"

I blinked. *That's right, coffee,* I thought. That's how it all began. With a cup of coffee . . . A silly grin spread over my face. Just thinking about the mouse you love can make you do that.

Meanwhile, Thea was staring at me like I was some kind of rodent science experiment. Suddenly, she groaned. "*Did you fall in love?*" she squeaked. "Is that why you're acting so strange?"

I sighed happily. "LOVE, isn't it wonderful?" I beamed. Then I pulled a wad of bills out of my pocket. I began counting them

Is anybody home?!

*I began counting the bills as if
they were petals on a flower.*

as if they were petals on a flower. "She loves me, she loves me not, she loves me, she loves me not . . ." I sang.

Thea rolled her eyes in disgust. "You'd better get your act together, big brother," she advised. "In case you've forgotten, you are *the publisher of a newspaper.* There's a ton of work to be done!"

I twirled my tail, lost in thought. *Work,* I thought **DREAMILY**. I wonder what kind of work the most beautiful mouse in the world does. She looked so smart. So polished. Maybe she was the head of her own **advertising agency**. Or perhaps she was an international supermodel.

I was so busy thinking about my *soul mouse* that I barely heard the knock on my door.

I'M IN L-O-V-E!

My secretary, Mousella MacMouser, came rushing in. She was pushing an enormouse **DICTIONARY** on wheels. "Mr. Stilton! We've got to call the printer! I just found five misspelled words in tomorrow's edition!" she squeaked.

I nodded at Mousella. "Yes, call the printer. Call the radio station. Call every mouse in

the city," I announced gleefully. "I want everyone to know. I'm in L-O-V-E!"

Mousella gave me a strange look. Then she took the dictionary and scurried out of the office. "Crazy, lovesick mouse," I heard her mumble before she left.

Just then, I heard music blasting in the hallway. I left my desk to see what was going on. It looked like a **WILD MOUSE PARTY**. Mice were laughing and hanging out at the water cooler. Two mice danced by me doing the TANGO. Another mouse was making paper airplanes. No one was doing any work.

Normally, I would be upset. I would tell everyone to get back to their desks. But today I didn't care. I was too happy. I was too excited. I was in love with a capital "L."

Thea shook her head. "When the boss is away, the mice will PLAY," she snorted.

Two minutes later, an elegant female mouse tapped me on the shoulder. She was dressed in a very expensive-looking cat-fur jacket and matching skirt.

"Who are you? What do you want?" I mumbled distractedly. I was busy doodling tiny hearts in my notebook.

"Who am I? Don't you recognize me? I'm

Kreamy O'Cheddar, your editor in chief! I've been working for you for the past twenty years!!!" she squeaked, sounding **ANNOYED**.

I looked up at her. "Ah, yes, you do look sort of familiar," I nodded. I glanced at her outfit. "She wears expensive clothes, too," I murmured, lost in thought. "I bet she looks fabumouse in cat fur. . . ."

By now, the whole office was staring at me. I heard them whispering among themselves. *Buzz, buzz . . .*

"He's lost it," someone mumbled.

"Talk about dizzy with love," someone else commented.

Suddenly, I noticed a picture on the front page of the paper.

Kreamy O'Cheddar

"That's her! That's her!" I shouted. I was so excited, I could hardly breathe. I read the caption under the picture: "The young countess *Stephanie von Sugarfur*, daughter of the renowned count Chester Cheesenip, arrived in town yesterday. The countess, who is staying at the Grand Cheddar Hotel, will be a guest at the embassy ball this coming Saturday."

I drew hearts

around the picture. I was grinning from ear to ear. "Stephanie! Ah, Stephanie!" I murmured.

My sister shook her head. "Geronimo, you're hopeless!" she smirked. "Absolutely **hopeless**!"

FIVE DOZEN RED ROSES

I left work and ran to the florist. I had to order flowers for Stephanie. Lots of flowers. And not just any **flowers**. Oh, no. A mouse as breathtaking as the countess deserved only the best. I settled on five dozen long-stemmed red roses.

The roses were perfect. Now I just had to *write* something on the card. "Mousey regards," I tried. No, maybe something more personal. I tore up the card. "Hugs and kisses," I wrote next. No, that wasn't right, either. *"Rodently yours,"* I scribbled. Hmm, that seemed a little too formal.

No, that wasn't right, either.

I stared into space. Then I noticed the florist staring back at me. Well, he wasn't just staring. He was shooting me dirty looks.

"Have you finished yet? You are **using up** all of my cards!" he squeaked. "Why don't you just write your name?"

"M-My name?" I asked in a daze.

"Yes, your signature! I take it  you do know your own name!" he burst out impatiently. Then he closed his eyes. "I need a vacation," he mumbled. "These lovesick mice are such nitwits!"

Normally, I would mind if some mouse called me a nitwit. But today, I couldn't care less. So what if I was acting like a nitwit? *Stephanie von Sugarfur* was worth it. Full of excitement, I signed the card. Then I stuck it under the silk bow tying up the gigantic bunch of red roses.

CHEESE-FLAVORED CHOCOLATES

I spent the whole evening waiting for the phone to ring. I was hoping the countess would call to thank me for the **flowers**. But the only thing that rang was my toaster oven's timer. I was so surprised. Why didn't she call me? Every now and then, I LIFTED THE RECEIVER to make sure the phone was working.

The next day, I raced to the candy store to buy some Cheesy Chews. Have you ever had a Cheesy Chew? They're the best **CHEESE-FLAVORED CHOCOLATES** in all

Trap stuck a paw in my new box of chocolates.

of New Mouse City. I decided on a ten-pound super-deluxe box.

As I was paying, my cousin Trap strode into the store. Yes, he is a mouse, too. But you could never call him quiet. In fact, he is one of the **LOUDEST** rodents I know. It's amazing we're related.

Now he stuck a paw in my new box of chocolates. "Who are these for?" he said, swallowing a Swiss caramel chocolate **IN ONE GULP**.

"No!" I yelled. "They're not for you!" But it was too late. He had already scarfed down half the box. Tears sprang to my eyes. My precious gift was **ruined**. I couldn't send the countess a half-eaten box of chocolates. Even if they were expensive Cheesy Chews. "**HOW COULD YOU**?" I scolded Trap. "That was a present!"

My cousin barely blinked. "No problemo, Cousinkins," he squeaked. "It's my **BIRTHDAY** next month. I'll just pretend this is a little gift from you to me."

I sighed. "Would you please give me another sealed box?" I asked the salesmouse.

Trap shook my paw. "Thanks, Gerry Berry!" he giggled, **TOSSING MORE CHOCOLATES INTO HIS MOUTH.** "By the way, Thea tells me you've got a new sweetheart. Want some advice?"

I rolled my eyes. The last mouse I'd take advice from is my cousin.

"Listen to me, Cousinkins," Trap advised. "Lady mice like a challenge. You've got to play it cool. Don't let her know you're interested."

A LACE
PAWKERCHIEF

Once again, I spent the night waiting for the telephone to ring. But the beautiful countess did **NOT** call. Then I had a horrible thought. What if she was allergic to roses? What if chocolate made her fur itch? My heart sank. I had to do something. I decided to go to her hotel.

I was too embarrassed to wait in the lobby. So I hid behind the bushes.

Suddenly, someone laid a paw on my shoulder. "Holey cheese!" I shrieked. But it was only my favorite nephew, Benjamin.

"Uncle Geronimo! What are you doing here?" he squeaked.

Right
then, I saw
her come out.

"*Shhhh*, little mousey,"
I murmured to Benjamin. I
stood up, trying to look casual.
The countess seemed to look right
through me. Then *she* dropped something.
It was a small lace pawkerchief.

I ran to pick it up. "E-Excuse me, I'm the douse from the miner. I mean, mouse from the diner," I stammered. "I'm the one who sent you the **red noses**. I mean, roses. The

one who sent you the sandy. I mean, candy.
It's me, Gilton, *Steronimo Gilton*!" I
know I was making no sense. But I couldn't
believe I was speaking with her again. After
all, who knew? She could be my one true
love. My best friend forever. Yes, she could
be the future Mrs. Geronimo Stilton!

The countess opened her eyes wide and
gazed at me. "Oh!" she breathed.

I gave her the pawkerchief. Then I tried to bow. Big mistake. I tripped and tumbled back into a rosebush. When I managed to stand up, roses were sticking out of my nose. I staggered off into the road. That's when I heard the roar of an engine. I looked up just in time to see a huge cream cheese truck headed right for me!

"**Help!!**" I shrieked.

The truck **STOPPED** within inches of my snout. Seconds later, an expensive sports car screeched to a halt in front of the hotel. A polished-looking mouse leaped out. He ran up to the countess and kissed her paw.

"My darling *Stephanie*!" he crooned. "They are all waiting for you at the ball!"

Then the two of them disappeared into the night.

The two of them disappeared into the night.

I TOLD YOU TO PLAY IT COOL!

The following morning, I dragged myself to the office. I was so depressed. The countess wasn't interested in me. She already had Mr. Flashy Sports Car Mouse. She probably laughed at my silly roses and threw my chocolates in the trash. Oh, how could I have been so foolish?

I doodled a string of **broken ♡ hearts** in my notebook. Then I began to sob loudly.

Thea marched into my office. She looked at my drawing and shook her head.

"She broke your heart, didn't she?" Thea demanded to know. "If you ask me, you should have played it cool."

I **sobbed** louder.

Minutes later, Trap stuck his head into the room. "What's with the waterworks, Cousinkins?" he asked. Thea pointed to the broken hearts. Trap rolled his eyes.

"I told you to play it cool!" he sneered.

Just then, a small rodent scurried through the door. It was my nephew Benjamin. He stared at the hearts in my notebook.

"Uncle, maybe you should have played it cool," he squeaked.

I moaned. Just thinking about the countess made me choke. How could I live without my soul mouse? My inspiration? My heart? I put my snout between my paws and cried like a rat stuck in a glue trap on Christmas Eve.

THE VALLEY OF THE CHEESETTES

That night, I slunk home. I dropped into my pawchair in front of the television. I usually don't watch a lot of TV. But I was feeling too sad to do anything else. I set a box of tissues out next to me. I knew I would need them. I just couldn't stop crying. It was like I had sprung a LEAK. Oh, why did I have to fall in love with that mouse?

Lost in my own thoughts, I barely heard the doorbell ring. "Who is it?" I mumbled. Why wasn't I allowed to suffer in peace?

Whoever it was didn't give up. I shuffled toward the door and opened it.

"Hey, there, big brother!" squeaked Thea. Trap and Benjamin were by her side.

"I'm really not up for company," I said with a sigh. I tried to close the door, but my cousin pushed his way inside.

"Listen, Cousinkins, We're here to cheer you up!" he declared, grinning. "After all, that is what relatives are for, isn't it?" He marched over to my megahuge fridge. "Got any cheddar balls?" he asked. "The old tummy's rumbling."

I jumped to my paws. My cousin had an endless appetite. He would eat me out of house and hole if I didn't stop him.

Luckily, Thea beat me to it. "No time for food," she told Trap, yanking him away by the tail. "We're here to cheer up Geronimo.

He looks like he's been eaten by a cat!"

She stuck a magazine under my snout.

"Read this!" she instructed.

World's Eighth Wonder Still a Mystery!

the headline declared.

The article said an **ancient** report had been found in New Mouse City's library. The report was written by the famouse explorer Richard Ratingbone. Ratingbone had journeyed to Butterfly Island in search of the legendary **VALLEY OF THE CHEESETTES**. The valley is said to be the Eighth Wonder of the World. Unfortunately, Ratingbone was not able to find it. Years later, explorers continue to search for the valley's secret entrance.

I dropped the paper, shuffled back to my pawchair, and SAT DOWN. "So why are you showing me this?" I asked wearily.

My cousin's grin spread from ear to ear. "Don't you get it, Germeister?" he squeaked. "We'll go in search of this cheesy valley place. Then we'll become **RICH** and *famouse*!"

I rolled my eyes. "First of all, Trap, it's the **VALLEY OF THE CHEESETTES**," I said. "And second of all, I'm just not up for a trip right now. I wouldn't be any fun at all." I sighed heavily. Then I stared blankly at the television screen. On it, two mice were holding paws and skipping off into the sunset. The female mouse looked just like the countess. I started **crying** like a sprinkler on high speed.

My family took the hint.

Disappointed, they let themselves out.

HOLD ON TIGHT!

The next day, Thea marched into my office. "Listen up, miserable mousey," she announced. "I've got the answer to all of your problems."

I looked up from my desk. My sister was grinning at me like she had just swallowed ten grilled cheese sandwiches. Uh-oh, I thought. That look could only mean one thing. Thea had some **CRAZY** and MYSTERIOUS scheme up her sleeve. My sister loves adventure. She probably wanted to take me rock climbing. Or even worse — skydiving.

Before I could squeak, she grabbed me by the paw. "Come on, **sad sack**!" she cried, dragging me out of the office.

A few minutes later, I found myself sitting

on the back of Thea's motorcycle. Did I mention my sister is a bit of a **DAREDEVIL**? She loves fast bikes. Fast cars. And fast boats. In fact, the only thing she doesn't like fast is her food. Those McRatburgers can be a little hard on a rodent's stomach.

Now I shut my eyes tight as we roared down the road. "Hold on **TIII IIGHT!**" Thea shrieked happily. The wind whipped by us. When we stopped, I stared down at my fur. It was a tangled mess. It would take me weeks to comb through it. Oh, how I hate motorcycles!

Just then, I sniffed the air. I looked around. We were parked in

a **dark** and *smelly* alley.

My sister pushed me off the bike and into a small doorway. "Someone is waiting for you on the tenth floor," she told me. "You'll have to take the stairs. There's no elevator. I'll wait down here with the bike."

What could I do? I had to go. My sister was only trying to help. Maybe I would meet a friendly psychiatrist on the tenth floor. Or a beautiful female mouse. That got me thinking about the countess.

Sobbing, I began to climb.

MADAME LOVE DOCTOR

I reached the tenth floor, out of breath. My heart was beating wildly in my chest. A sign on the door in front of me read,

Suddenly, it all became clear. My sister was sending me to a fortune-teller. Yes, some wacky mouse who claims to tell the future. I groaned. I didn't have time for this

Then the fortune-teller uncovered a crystal ball.

mumbo jumbo. I had my whole day planned out. First I would feel sorry for myself. Then I would cry me a **river of tears**. Then I would float home and cry some more. Yes, I had an important schedule to keep.

I was about to leave when the door opened with a creak. I caught sight of a **DUSTY** room. It smelled like incense and burning candles.

"Come in," said a feeble voice. "I've been waiting for you."

How strange, I thought. I could have sworn I had heard that voice before. But before I could figure it out, the voice continued. "Come in, Mr. Stilton," it murmured. "And bring your broken little heart with you."

I **FROZE**. How did she know my name? And how did she know about the countess?

In the corner of the room, I saw a strange

figure. She was wearing a long, flowing dress. Her head was covered by a **FADED** pawkerchief. The room was so dark, *I couldn't make out her face.*

The fortune-teller pushed me into a chair. Then she uncovered a CRYSTAL BALL.

I almost giggled. Maybe next she would try to read the lines on my paw. It was all so very silly. I wanted to leave, but right then, the fortune-teller began to whisper.

"I see roses. A whole van of roses," she murmured. "And chocolates. Gourmet cheese-flavored chocolates. Yum, yum."

My jaw hit the ground. My blood ran **COLD**. My fur stood up in shock. Did this rodent really have magical powers?

The fortune-teller sniggered with delight. I guess she liked surprising her clients.

"Roses aren't enough, neither are chocolates," she went on. "You need much more to win over this mouse, Germeister."

I blinked. "Germeister?" I murmured. How very strange. Why did this rodent seem **SOOO** familiar to me?

She coughed, then continued. "Are you willing to do anything to make **your true love** fall at your paws?" she asked.

Hope made my heart beat faster. I nodded "yes" so hard that my eyes rattled in my fur. I leaned closer.

The fortune-teller told me I needed to do

something **extraordinary**. Something no mouse had ever done before. Something so amazing it would make me famouse. Then *Stephanie von Sugarfur* would be sure to notice me.

I scratched my head. "S-S-Something amazing?" I stammered. "But I'm just an average mouse. I run a newspaper. I'm not an **EXPLORER**."

The fortune-teller took a closer look at her crystal ball. "But I see that some very clever rodents want you to go on a trip with them. You must go. It will be an amazing success!" she predicted.

I chewed my whiskers. I was planning on

sulking in front of the TV set all weekend. Still, my family would be so **happy** if I joined them on their trip.

"Do you really think it will work?" I asked.

"Of course, you cheesebrain!" she shrieked. "Madame Love Doctor knows all. Now go home, pack your suitcase, and be off!"

Then she held out her **fleshy paw**. "By the way, that will be two hundred dollars."

I nearly fell off my chair. Two hundred dollars! What a business. Maybe I should buy my own crystal ball. I could be rich! As if in a dream, I took out my wallet. **QUICKER** than a cat with a ball of yarn, she snatched up the cash.

I headed out the door.

"And don't forget to play it cool!"

the fortune-teller called after me.

I stopped. Now, where had I heard those words recently? Before I could remember, a paw grabbed my shoulder. It was Thea.

"How did it go?" she asked.

I told her what the fortune-teller had said. About the roses. About the chocolates. And about the AMAZING TRIP that would make me famous. "So I guess I will go with you," I finished.

For some reason, Thea didn't look too surprised. We roared off on her bike.

"Hang on to your whiskers!" my sister cried.

I was hanging on to more than my whiskers. I was hanging on for *dear life*!

WE'RE OFF!

Minutes later, we reached the airport. Thea had refused to stop at my place for my suitcase. She was afraid I would change my mind. Plus, she said I take too long packing. I don't know why. Don't all rodents sort their clothes by color, size, and fabric?

Benjamin was already waiting for us at the airport. Trap showed up a few minutes later. "Don't leave without me!" *HE PANTED, OUT OF BREATH*.

Thea was already giving instructions to the mechanics. Did I tell you my sister flies her very own plane? A pink one with flowers! She's totally into it. She can do loops. She can do spins. She can even fly upside down. Last year, she won Mouse Island's Fearless Furs Flight Competition. It was amazing to watch. But I was happy when she landed in one piece.

As for me, I'm afraid to fly. Mice look like tiny ants when you're up in the sky. My teeth began to chatter just thinking about taking off. "M-M-Maybe we should wait

until tomorrow," I stammered, looking nervously at Thea's plane.

My sister rolled her eyes. "Get over it, **GERRY BERRY**!" she scolded. "You're such a scaredy mouse."

She turned to greet all of her friends. "Hey, there, Squeaks! How's it going, Sniffer?" she called.

The male rodents stopped and stared when Thea went by. I wish I had her luck when it came to love. My sister has more admirers than a mouse who just won the lottery.

Just then, a furry rodent wearing a parachuting outfit approached Thea. "Would you like to, um, go for, um, a jump together?" he stammered, blushing.

My sister giggled and fluttered her eyelashes. "Sounds **fabumouse**," she murmured sweetly. "But I can't today."

The parachutist shot me a dirty look. I guess he thought I was Thea's date for the day.

I felt sorry for him. I knew exactly how he felt. Rejected with a capital "**R**." Thea took that moment to pass on some advice. Actually, it was the same old advice I'd been listening to for days. "See?" she whispered. "You have to play it cool. Then you'll be irresistible."

I was thinking about what Thea had said when a paw stroked my shoulder. "Geronimo," a high-pitched voice crooned. "It's me, Stephanie von Sugarfur."

My heart **BEAT** wildly. So much for playing it cool. I would ask her out to dinner. I would ask her to the movies. I would ask her to *marry me*! Excited, I turned around. But instead of seeing Stephanie's sweet snout I was staring right at my cousin Trap. He threw his arms

around me and began to kiss the air.

"Hee, hee, heee!" my annoying cousin snickered. "**GERRY BERRY**, you are just so easy to fool. What a total NINCOMPOOP!"

I'M NOT FEELING TOO GOOD

I climbed into the plane with shaky paws. I checked my seat belt buckle ten times. I located the nearest exit. I made sure there was an inflatable life vest under my seat.

"Up, up and away!" Thea squeaked as the plane's wheels left the ground.

My **CLAWS** dug into the seat. I really do hate flying. Maybe even more than I hate pickled blue cheese sandwiches. I mean, why would you ruin a delicious cheese with pickle juice?

Trap's voice broke into my thoughts. "Thea, how long have you been flying?" he smirked. "Two days, a week? It doesn't look to me like you can do any tricks."

Thea turned to glare at my cousin. "How dare you?" she shrieked. Minutes later, the plane soared straight into the sky, then dove down in a loop.

I covered my eyes with my paws. "Oh, no! No tricks!" I cried. But, as usual, no one was listening to me.

"That's it?" Trap shouted. "That's the whole show?"

Thea was fuming. I opened my eyes long enough to see steam pouring from her ears. Before I knew it, we were rolling through the air. Then Thea put the plane into a tailspin. I thought I was going to lose my lunch.

"I'm not feeling too good . . ." I murmured in a whisper.

I grabbed an air sickness bag.

Behind me, Trap kept squeaking away. "Really, that's all you can do, Thea?" he **scoffed**. "Maybe you should step aside. I bet I could fly this thing with my eyes closed."

By now, my eyes were sealed shut. Oh, why did I get into a plane with these two nuts? I should have known this would happen. My sister and my cousin are like mold and cheese. They're just not good together.

"Here comes the best part. The death loop!" my sister squeaked. I began to **sob**.

The plane flipped in the air again and again.

"**YIIIIPPEEEEE!**" shouted my sister.

"B-B-Big deal!" stammered Trap.

I didn't say a word. Instead, **I fainted**. Trap brought me back by holding a piece of smelly cheese under my nose.

"Please, no more," I cried, still shaking.

"Oh, don't be such a coward, Geronimoid," my sister scolded. "We're almost there anyway."

Minutes later, we dropped down onto a runway. Tears sprang to my eyes. But this time, they were tears of joy. I was alive!

RISKY RODENT TRAVELS

We climbed off the plane. A cute female mouse wearing a bikini greeted us. She hung a garland of flowers around each of our necks. "Welcome to Sweet Rose Island!" she squeaked.

Outside the airport, we headed for the rental cars. That's when I spotted a dented old jeep with the words RISKY RODENT TRAVELS painted on the side. Suddenly, my stomach lurched. Why did I have a feeling that jeep was for us?

I was right. Thea jumped on board in a flash. She and Trap had to haul me on kicking and squeaking. Oh, how had I gotten myself into this mess?

Thea sat behind the wheel. Then she turned the key. The jeep roared off with a

SQUEAL OF TIRES.

The journey seemed to last forever. Finally, the car stopped with a jolt. I gathered my last bit of strength and crawled out.

To my horror, I realized we were at a harbor. Thea immediately jumped into a DANGEROUS-LOOKING pencil-thin speedboat. The others followed. But not me. Not this time. I dug in my heels.

"I'm not getting in!" I shrieked. "Boats are bad enough. But I cannot get on a speedboat! It's just too scary!"

Just then, Trap let out a squeak. "Geronimo, look!" he cried, pointing to the bottom of the boat. "Someone left a copy of *Ratty Potter*. And it's signed by the author!"

For a moment, I forgot where I was. I love *Ratty Potter*. He's a young mouse wizard who has all of these *incredible adventures*. I have read all the books in the series. It would be so amazing to get a copy signed by the author.

I leaned over to get a better look into the boat. And that's when Trap grabbed my tail. He yanked me into the boat. I had been tricked!

Thea started the engine.

"**Heeelp!** I'm being mousenapped!" I shouted, terrified.

But no one was around to hear me. No one except my family, that is. And they were

the ones doing the mousenapping!

"Relax, big brother!" squeaked Thea, fastening her seat belt. "We're off to Butterfly Island! Get ready for an amazing time!"

THE TEN STAGES OF SEASICKNESS

1. *At the port*

Do you suffer from motion sickness? I do.

I get sick on boats. I get sick on planes. I get sick in cars. It's really the most awful feeling. First my ears begin to buzz. Then my tail twitches. Then my eyes cross. Then my stomach lurches. Finally, I turn as pale as a slice of mozzarella.

When we reached Butterfly Island, Thea, Trap, and Benjamin had to carry me off the boat.

2. *On the gangplank*

3. *On the ladder*

4. *By the shore*

5. *Away from the port*

"I'm not getting on any plane, boat, or car," I shouted. "Ever again!"

Thea stared at me with an innocent expression. "Who said you have to?" she smiled.

"You mean . . . no planes?" I asked, looking around.

10. *In a storm*

"**NO** planes," she replied.

"**NO** boats?" I continued, still not convinced.

"Not a one," she agreed.

"**NO** cars? **NO** Trains?" I pressed in disbelief.

9. *On high seas*

Thea just kept shaking her head.

At last, I heaved a sigh of relief. Thank goodness, there would be

8. *On short waves*

6. *In open seas*

7. *On long waves*

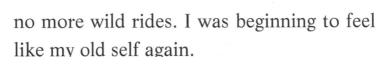

no more wild rides. I was beginning to feel like my old self again.

"Which way do we go now? I asked cheerfully. "Where is this famouse **VALLEY OF THE CHEESETTES**?"

Thea waved her paw in one direction. "Oh, it's right around here," she answered.

I unfolded a map. That's when I noticed something. The whole island was shaped like a giant butterfly! *How very odd,* I thought.

I looked around me. There was green everywhere. Green trees, green bushes, green grass. This place was a gardener's dream. I stepped forward into the high grass. Then I stopped. A strange feeling came over me. There was something WRONG with this picture. I just couldn't quite put my paw on it.

Behind me, I heard Trap humming a silly

The whole island was shaped like a giant butterfly.

tune. It was from some popular TV show. My cousin loves cartoons. He knows all the theme songs by heart.

At that moment, I realized what was wrong with the island. There were **NO** rodents. There were **NO** buzzing insects. There were **NO** chirping birds. There were **NO** sounds at all. Except for Trap, it was quieter than the Cheddarton Library when mean Mrs. Hushermouse is working.

I felt a shiver run up my tail. My paws began to shake. My heart started to race.

What kind of an island was this?

WE MARCH ON!

Trap snatched the map from me. He studied it for a few seconds. Then he clapped his paws together.

"**FOLLOW ME!**" he ordered, leading the way.

We started marching.

We marched for one hour.

We marched for two hours.

We marched for three hours.

The sun began to set. We had been marching for at least five hours!

Soon it was dark. I could barely see my nose on the end of my snout. Did I mention I'm afraid of the dark? I'm also not the most in-shape mouse on the block. In fact, I guess you could say I'm in no shape. No shape for running or jogging or even fast walking.

"Can't we take a break now?" **I begged**. But Trap insisted we were almost there.

I groaned. My paws were covered in blisters. The backpack Thea had loaned me weighed more than my uncle Cheesebelly after Christmas dinner. I felt like I had been run over by **A FIFTY-POUND BLOCK** of Swiss. Even my whiskers were sweating.

Just then, I had the most horrible thought.

"Trap, are you sure you know where you're going?" I asked my cousin.

He whirled around, annoyed. "Of course I'm sure! We go forward!" squeaked Trap.

I thought about that for a moment.

"But where are we headed?" I inquired NERVOUSLY.

My cousin stamped his paws. "Are your ears filled with cheese?!" he shrieked. "*FORWARD* means forward, doesn't it?!" He snorted in disgust.

At that moment, my sister chimed in. "Where exactly are we headed, Trap?" she asked.

My cousin waved his paw in the air. "Well, it looks like we are in the middle of a forest, right?" he said, pointing to all of the trees surrounding us. "And the sea is behind us, right? So I figure if we keep going forward we're bound to get somewhere, right?"

My sister put her paws on her hips. "So basically you are telling us you have no idea

NO IDEA?

where we are???" she shrieked in a fit of anger.

The two of them were soon at each other's throats.

I'VE NEVER MET A
RODENT LIKE YOU

We decided to set up camp for the night.

I was exhausted. As soon as the camp's fire burned out, I fell into a **DeeP, VeRY DeeP** sleep.

I dreamed I was having a romantic dinner with *Stephanie von Sugarfur*. She was smiling at me like I was the best thing since individually wrapped mozzarella balls.

"Oh, Geronimo, you're such a wonderful mouse!" she squeaked. "I've never met a rodent like you."

I held her paw. I was so happy. I could sit and stare into her eyes all night.

But suddenly, I woke up with a start.

Someone was shaking me by the shoulder.
"Who is it? Leave me alone!" I mumbled.
It was Benjamin. "*Shhh,* Uncle, you have
to see this," he whispered, tugging on my
paw. "Come with me. But SHHH, don't
make any noise."

JUST LIKE A SLICE OF CHEESE!

Benjamin brought me to the mouth of a cave. Then he pointed toward a small butterfly flying over our heads. It was yellow with TINY HOLES on its wings. It looked just like a slice of cheese!

"How extraordinary!" I exclaimed. "I've never seen such a butterfly! Maybe it comes from the mysterious valley."

"That's what I was thinking, Uncle," whispered Benjamin. "The Valley of the Cheesettes!"

The small butterfly was flitting about in front of us. It seemed to be inviting us to follow it.

How very strange, I thought. Why would a butterfly want to hang out with a couple of mice? Didn't he have any butterfly friends?

Just then, the butterfly slipped into the cave. Without thinking, Benjamin and I followed it.

I CAN'T SEE A WHISKER!

The cave was **DAMP** and dark. I couldn't see my own whiskers in front of my snout! It was so dark, I lost track of Benjamin. "Where are you, Nephew?" I cried in a panic, my words echoing in the dark.

"I'm right behind you, Uncle," Benjamin's voice answered again and again.

We held tails so we wouldn't lose track of each other.

At that moment, I saw a terrifying sight. Two spooky yellow eyes were looking at us in the dark. They probably belonged to a mouse-eating monster!

"**RANCID RAT HAIRS!**" I shrieked. My voice echoed in the deep,

The butterfly's wings glowed in the dark.

dark cave. My **BLOOD** froze in my veins. My whiskers started to tremble. "S-S-Something is w-w-watching us," I told Benjamin. I didn't want to scare him. I mean, he's only nine years old. Still, I thought he should know if we were about to be eaten.

But instead of squeaking, my nephew just giggled. "Don't be afraid, Uncle. Those aren't eyes," he explained, "they're the butterfly's wings. They glow in the dark."

I looked closer. Benjamin was right. It was the butterfly after all. I felt a little silly for being such a scaredy mouse. But luckily my nephew adores me. He would never make fun of his *favorite uncle*.

The butterfly led us deeper and deeper into the darkness. Now we had to follow it. Its wings were our only light.

I'M AFRAID OF THE DARK!

The cave grew narrower and narrower. I guess you could say it was shaped a bit like a slice of cheese. At the end, there was a tiny **HOLE**. The butterfly **disappeared** through it.

I tried to follow. But the hole was much too small for me. It was too small for any adult mouse. Only a small mouse Benjamin's size could fit through it.

"LET ME GO, UNCLE!" he whispered. *"I'LL BE CAREFUL. PLUS, I BROUGHT MY CAMERA. I CAN TAKE LOTS OF PICTURES."*

I put my paw around my nephew. I made him promise ten times to be careful. Then he kissed my snout and disappeared through the tiny opening.

I sat down and waited. Every now and then I would peek into the hole and squeak,

**"Benjamin!
Benjamin!!!
Benjamin!!!"**

Unfortunately, I'd forgotten my watch. I had no idea how much time had gone by. Was it an hour? Was it a day? Was it forever and a day? I started to **WORRY** about Benjamin. He was just a little thing. What if something happened to him? I would never forgive myself for letting him go. Oh, how could I have been so foolish? I

should have never let him disappear into that hole. Now I was stuck in this creepy dark cave all alone. "Benjamin, come back!" I sobbed. "I'm afraid of the dark!"

GOOD-BYE, BUTTERFLY!

Finally, I heard a rustling sound. It was Benjamin! I was so happy, I began squeaking like the head cheerleader at a ratball game. "I was worried about you!" I cried, giving him a hug. I was worried about myself, too. One more minute alone in the **dark** and I'd have gone completely nuts.

"Uncle!" Benjamin cried now, grabbing my paw. "I saw it! I saw the Valley of the Cheesettes! *It was unbelievable! It was amazing!* It was more beautiful than a room full of cheddar bars!"

"I'm so **PROUD** of you, Benjamin," I squeaked. And I was. That nephew of mine really was one brave little rodent.

I peeked through the narrow hole, trying to catch a glimpse of the valley. But it was too dark. "Don't worry, Uncle,"

BENJAMIN TOLD ME.

"I took lots of pictures." It was time to go. I couldn't wait to tell the others our news. "Good-bye, Butterfly!" Benjamin called over his shoulder. "Thanks for the tour!"

We headed back through the cave. I followed a small light up ahead. It was the entrance to the cave. Then, suddenly, a low RUMBLING shook the walls. Rocks began to crumble down around us.

"Cheese niblets!" I shrieked. "It's an

avalanche! Run quick, Nephew, or we'll be trapped inside!"

Just then, an enormouse boulder struck Benjamin, and he fainted. I was terrified. I chewed my whiskers. I twisted my tail up in knots. I cried twenty buckets of tears. Then a rock hit me on the head. It must have knocked some sense into me. This was no time to feel sorry for myself. I had to save my nephew!

With a GROAN, I lifted Benjamin onto my shoulder. Did I mention I'm not the strongest mouse on the block? Still, fear must have given me strength. I raced for the exit like an Olympic trackrat champion.

Just as I ran out of the cave, a huge boulder blocked the entrance.

Right then, Benjamin opened his eyes.

"Uncle Geronimo, thank you for saving

my life," he grinned. "You're a real **HERO**!"

I smiled back. I wasn't about to tell him how scared I had been. After all, it wouldn't be nice to disappoint him. "Don't mention it," I shrugged, untwisting my tail.

Back at camp, my *dear* relatives Thea and Trap were busy. No, they weren't busy worrying about us. They were busy snoring away!

"Wake up, **wake uuup**!" Benjamin shrieked. "We found the Eighth Wonder of the World!

The two sleepyheads were up in a flash.

HUNDREDS, THOUSANDS, MILLIONS OF BUTTERFLIES

Benjamin told us all about his incredible adventure. It seems our little butterfly friend had taken him to the top of a mountain peak. It overlooked a valley. The valley was long and wide. It glowed in a bright yellow light. It was so bright at first that Benjamin covered his eyes. But when he opened them, he saw the most amazing thing. There wasn't really a light at all. There were just yellow butterflies. Hundreds and thousands and millions of butterflies!

"And when they flapped their wings, it smelled just like cheese!" Benjamin exclaimed.

Hundreds and thousands and millions of butterflies!

The butterflies were very friendly. They even sat on Benjamin's nose.

"I took lots of pictures," he finished. "I even took one of myself using the self-timer. Wait till you see it!"

Thea clapped her paws. "This is **fabumouse**!" she shrieked. "We're all going to be famous. I'll write the best story ever. It will sell like hot cheese buns in a blizzard!"

Trap jumped to his paws. "I've got an even better idea!" he announced. "First we catch a whole bunch of those butterflies. Then we smash them into a book. Then we FRAME each one. We'll make a bundle!"

I shook my head. Only my rotten cousin would think of squishing those beautiful butterflies. He would do anything for money.

Benjamin looked horrified. He turned to me with tears in his eyes.

"Don't worry, Nephew," I soothed. "No one is going to lay a paw on the butterflies." I shot Trap a look. "Besides," I added. "There was an avalanche. The entrance to the cave is blocked forever."

Thea agreed we didn't need the real butterflies. BENJAMIN'S PICTURES WOULD TELL THE WHOLE STORY. She took the camera and rolls of film from my nephew. Then she carefully slipped them into a plastic bag. Those PHOTOGRAPHS were more precious than cheese. They were the only proof of our discovery.

Trap insisted on carrying the bag. I wasn't surprised. My cousin likes to feel important.

"Well, my work here is done. I found the **VALLEY OF THE CHEESETTES**," he declared. "Now, let's go home!"

I was too tired to correct him. Besides, we all knew Benjamin had really found the valley.

We packed up our stuff and headed home. *The trip was long and painful.* I poked myself in the eye on the speedboat. I was trying to cover my glasses. I didn't want to see the scary waves. Then I sprained my ankle jumping out of the jeep. Thea drove so *fast*, I just had to get out. And I fainted on the airplane. We hadn't even taken off. I guess just thinking about my sister's tricks up in the air was enough to do me in. The only thing that kept me going was the countess. Yes, *adoring and sweet* Stephanie von Sugarfur. Soon I

*Thea carefully slipped the camera and rolls
of film into a plastic bag.*

would be **famouse**. She wouldn't be able to resist me.

I'll come back a hero! I giggled to myself. When the countess saw me on **Mouse TV**, she'd fall at my paws!

THIS IS A JOKE, ISN'T IT?

At last, we reached New Mouse City. I was so happy to be home. I couldn't wait to take a long, hot bath. I couldn't wait to sleep in my comfy bed. But mostly, I couldn't wait to see *Stephanie von Sugarfur*. Still, there was no time to relax yet. As soon as we landed, we hurried to the office. We wanted to get the paper ready. It would be an amazing breaking story. We had found the Eighth Wonder of the World! I could hardly believe it myself.

Thea began to make lots of phone calls. "Yes, yes, **darling**, I've already written a thrilling article," she exclaimed. "Of course there will be pictures. Tons and tons of pictures. You'll see the stunning valley. You'll see the gorgeous butterflies. I've got the photos right here in the office." She turned to my cousin and winked.

For some reason, Trap was looking **A LITTLE PALE**. He flopped onto a chair. Sweat was dripping down his fur. Maybe he was just overexcited. I was excited, too. It wasn't every day you became **famouse**!

My sister hung up. Then she turned to Trap. "OK, Cousin, give me those pictures," she demanded. "We've got to get them developed right away!"

Trap sunk deeper into his chair. "Um, well, I, um, might have lost them," he said, then smiled nervously.

My sister's jaw hit the ground. Her whiskers started to tremble. Steam poured from her ears. She narrowed her eyes at my cousin.

"This is one of your silly jokes, right?" she shrieked.

I stared at Trap. I had a funny feeling in the pit of my stomach. For once, my prankster cousin was not joking.

Trap managed to smile at my sister. "Well, I might have left them at the camp," he explained. "Or maybe I dropped them on the beach. Or I could have left them on the speedboat. Or maybe they fell out of the jeep. We did hit a lot of potholes, you know."

Thea tried to grab him by the throat. But he was too quick. So she **CHASED** him around the desk, squeaking at the top of her lungs.

I tried to calm them down. "Take it easy, it's not that bad," I offered. Uh oh. Wrong thing to say. Thea stopped RUNNING AFTER Trap. Now she was coming after me.

One thing you should know about my sister — she has an awful **TEMPER**. Once I ran over her Furry Fieldmouse doll with my tricycle. It was an accident. I mean, I was only a mouslet at the time. Thea got so

mad she smashed my trike to pieces. The only thing left was the horn.

Now she turned to me in a rage. "It's not that **bad**?" she shrieked. "How are we ever going to prove we found the Valley of the Cheesettes?"

Before I could think, Benjamin piped up. "Wait a minute, Auntie!" he cried. "I've got an idea."

He lifted his red hat. A small yellow butterfly FLEW OUT. It sat down on his shoulder.

"She must have hidden under my hat when we were in the cave," Benjamin said, grinning. "Isn't she cute? I call her Cheesette."

She was fascinating. She was bright yellow with holes like a slice of Swiss. A cheesy smell filled the air around her.

I watched the small butterfly fly around Benjamin!

Thea broke into a wide smile. "That's it!" she shouted. "We don't need pictures to prove we found the Valley of the Cheesettes. We have our own Cheesette right here!"

AND I MEAN
EVERYTHING!

"Hello, am I squeaking to Geronimo Stilton? The national **hero**? The famouse publisher? One of the mice who discovered the Cheesette butterfly?" said a voice.

I cleared my throat. "Yes, I am *Geronimo Stilton*," I began.

It was the next day. I was back in the office. I had been getting phone calls all

morning from reporters. It seemed my family and I had become famouse overnight. Now everyone wanted to know everything about us. And I mean everything! They wanted to know what kind of cheese I liked best. They wanted to know what kind of **fur brush** I used. They even wanted to know what kind of underwear I wore. It was crazy! My calendar was booked with interviews on *TV*. At the rate things were going, I wouldn't be free until next Christmas!

Just then, my secretary, Mousella, came charging in.

"Mr. Stilton, the phones are ringing off the hook!" she shouted. "The operator has quit. The fax machine is spitting out paper. And the computers are bursting with e-mail

messages!" She paused to catch her breath. "By the way," she continued. "Did you know there is a Geronimo Stilton fan club on the Internet?"

I sighed. Being famouse wasn't easy. Plus, the reporters had told me that an unmarried hero was the most POPULAR kind. Now every female mouse in New Mouse City was out to meet me. I was more popular than a grilled cheese sandwich at a weight loss clinic.

Suddenly, we heard a **rumble**. Mousella let out a shriek. "Your female admirers have broken into the building. They are about to storm the office!" she cried. "But don't worry, Boss. I'll get rid of them. Maybe I can throw them a hunk of cheese or something." She raced off with a determined look on her snout.

I shook my head. Then I stared out the

I LOVE GERONIMO STIL

window. Up in the sky, I spotted a plane carrying a banner. It read, *I LOVE GERONIMO STILTON!!!*

Right then, my cousin Trap strode into the room. He winked at me. "Guess what, Gerrykins," he said. "I have a surprise for you. And it's right behind this door."

I GROANED. I really wasn't in the mood for one of my cousin's tricks. "I don't have time for fun and games, Trap," I said. "I'm trying to get rid of these female admirers. They won't leave me alone."

My cousin giggled. "Come on **GERRY**

BeRRY, just come open the door," he insisted. "The fortune-teller was right. You'll like this surprise."

I scratched my fur. I thought only Thea had known about the fortune-teller. How strange. Still, what had that fortune-teller told me? She had said I would become famouse. Well, that had certainly come true. And after I became famouse, she said a certain mouse would fall in love with me. Madly in love.

Could it be true?

I SAID NO

I opened the door. And there she was. My beautiful, charming, sweet-smelling countess, *Stephanie von Sugarfur*. Only now, for some reason, she didn't seem so amazing anymore.

She sauntered up to me. "Oh, Geronimo, darling," she whispered. "I'm so glad you're home. Thank you so much for the roses. And the chocolates were delightful."

I blinked. Oh, yes, now I remembered. I had sent the countess flowers and that huge box of candy. How

STRANGE. It seemed like ages ago. So much had happened to me since then.

"I want to hear all about your trip," Stephanie went on. "Every last detail!"

I twirled my tail. I had been talking to reporters all morning. I just wasn't in the mood to tell the whole story again. "Well, we went and then we came back," I mumbled. "It was no big deal."

The countess frowned. I could tell she was waiting for me to fall all over her. But the truth was, I suddenly wasn't interested in her anymore. Oh, she was still a beautiful mouse. But my **heart** wasn't beating **WILDLY** like before. My paws weren't **sweating**. And I didn't feel the least bit **dizzy** when I looked at her. So I told her. I didn't love her anymore.

Stephanie turned pale. I think no one had

ever turned her down before. She was used to getting her mouse.

First she yelled at me. Then she cried. Then she tried **inviting** me to a dinner party at the mayor's mansion. But I said no. Want to know why? I couldn't care less.

Maybe I was just tired. Or maybe I was just tired of the countess. Now that I'd helped discover the Eighth Wonder of the World, she didn't seem so special anymore. Oh, well. I guess that's *love* for you. One minute you're in it. The next minute, you're not.

I guess that's love for you....

HELLO?
GERRYKINS, DEAR . . .

That night, I was so happy to be home. **"*ALONE AT LAST*,"** I said with a sigh. I unplugged my phone. Being famouse was harder than I'd thought. Reporters called me all day long. And my female admirers were everywhere. They followed me to breakfast. They followed me to lunch. I was tired of mice staring at me while I ate. All of those beady little eyes watching my every move. They **giggled** when I slurped my soup. They sighed when I dropped my napkin. It was enough to make a mouse quit eating altogether.

I decided I needed to unwind. I made myself a yummy mozzarella milk shake.

Then I took a steamy hot bubble bath. I had just climbed out of the tub when my cell phone rang.

"Hello," I squeaked, annoyed. I wasn't really in the mood for chatting. All I wanted to do was *relax*. All by myself.

"Gerrykins, dear, it's your beloved sister," Thea's voice shouted. "I wanted to invite you to my place. Will you come? OK, I'll be waiting. Byyyeee!"

I stamped my paw. "No, wait a minute!" I shrieked. "I don't want to go out!"

But it was too late. She had already hung up.

I dragged myself to my sister's place. She lived close by. You probably think I am one lazy mouse. But I'm not. I just needed one lazy night.

Of course, now I was stuck waiting outside my sister's front door. *She better make this quick,* I thought. I knocked on the door. Inside, I could hear lots of excited giggles.

Then someone murmured, **"Shhh!"**

Everything fell silent.

I pushed on the door. It opened. I blinked. The room was completely dark.

"Anyone home?" I asked warily.

SURPRISE! SURPRISE!

Suddenly, all the lights came on. "There he is, that's my brother, Geronimo Stilton!" Thea shouted.

Thirty-eight female mice began to shriek.

"Geronimo! Geronimo Stilton! We love you!" they cried.

I felt faint. My **heart** began to pound. My whiskers shook. *NO, this is not happening,* I told myself. Not on my do-what-I-want night. Not on my pig-out-on-cheese night. Not on my BE-BY-MYSELF night. Maybe I am just having a bad dream, I decided. Yes, that must be it. I tried closing my eyes. I tried practicing some meditation. I tried sneaking out the front door. But before I could escape, Thea grabbed my paw.

"Sit there at the head of the table, big brother," she instructed. "My friends here want you to tell them all about your trip." Then she leaned close to my ear. "And you better make it good!" she whispered.

Meanwhile, Thea's friends were hanging all over me. I could hardly move.

Geronimo,

"You're my **HERO**!" a honey-colored mouse squeaked.

"I want to know everything about your trip. And about *you*!" a furry gray mouse winked.

"You are much *cuter* than your picture!" a tawny mouse whispered.

Thea fluffed up her fur. She was so proud of herself. She loved being in charge. Plus, having me as a brother had made her more popular than ever.

I looked around. My admirers were everywhere. They stroked my fur. They pinched my tail. They stared deeply into my eyes.

Finally, I couldn't take it anymore. I just had to get away. I took off like a shot. The mice charged after me. I flung open the door to a closet and **LOCKED** it behind me.

"Geronimo! Come out!" squeaked my admirers. "We love you!"

I rested my head on my paws. Then I sighed.

Oh, well.

I guess that's love for you. . . .

I locked myself in a closet.

ABOUT THE AUTHOR

Born in New Mouse City, Mouse Island, Geronimo Stilton is Rattus Emeritus of Mousomorphic Literature and of Neo-Ratonic Comparative Philosophy. For the past twenty years, he has been running *The Rodent's Gazette*, New Mouse City's most widely read daily newspaper.

Stilton was awarded the Ratitzer Prize for his scoop on *The Curse of the Cheese Pyramid*. He has also received the Andersen 2000 Prize for Personality of the Year. One of his bestsellers won the 2002 eBook Award for world's best ratlings' electronic book. His works have been published all over the globe.

In his spare time, Mr. Stilton collects antique cheese rinds and plays golf. But what he most enjoys is telling stories to his nephew Benjamin.

Don't miss any of my other fabumouse adventures!

#1 Lost Treasure of the Emerald Eye

#2 The Curse of the Cheese Pyramid

#3 Cat and Mouse in a Haunted House

#4 I'm Too Fond of My Fur!

#5 Four Mice Deep in the Jungle

#6 Paws Off, Cheddarface!

and coming soon

#7 Red Pizzas for a Blue Count

#8 Attack of the Bandit Cats

#9 A Fabumouse Vacation for Geronimo

#11 It's Halloween, You 'Fraidy Mouse!

Want to read my next adventure?
It's sure to be a fur-raising experience!

IT'S HALLOWEEN, YOU 'FRAIDY MOUSE!

Crispy cheese treats! It was Halloween, the spookiest day of the year, and my nephew Benjamin had dragged me to a graveyard to do research for my newest book. There I met Creepella von Cacklefur, a very spooky mouse who — yikes! — tried to lock me up in her coffin! Oh, how would a 'fraidy mouse like me ever survive the year's scariest holiday?

The Rodent's Gazette

1. Main Entrance
2. Printing presses (where the books and newspaper are printed)
3. Accounts department
4. Editorial room (where the editors, illustrators, and designers work)
5. Geronimo Stilton's office
6. Storage space for Geronimo's books

Map of New Mouse City

1. Industrial Zone
2. Cheese Factories
3. Angorat International Airport
4. WRAT Radio and Television Station
5. Cheese Market
6. Fish Market
7. Town Hall
8. Snotnose Castle
9. The Seven Hills of Mouse Island
10. Mouse Central Station
11. Trade Center
12. Movie Theater
13. Gym
14. Catnegie Hall
15. Singing Stone Plaza
16. The Gouda Theater
17. Grand Hotel
18. Mouse General Hospital
19. Botanical Gardens
20. Cheap Junk for Less (Trap's store)
21. Parking Lot
22. Mouseum of Modern Art
23. University and Library
24. *The Daily Rat*
25. *The Rodent's Gazette*
26. Trap's House
27. Fashion District
28. The Mouse House Restaurant
29. Environmental Protection Center
30. Harbor Office
31. Mousidon Square Garden
32. Golf Course
33. Swimming Pool
34. Blushing Meadow Tennis Courts
35. Curlyfur Island Amusement Park
36. Geronimo's House
37. New Mouse City Historic District
38. Public Library
39. Shipyard
40. Thea's House
41. New Mouse Harbor
42. Luna Lighthouse
43. The Statue of Liberty

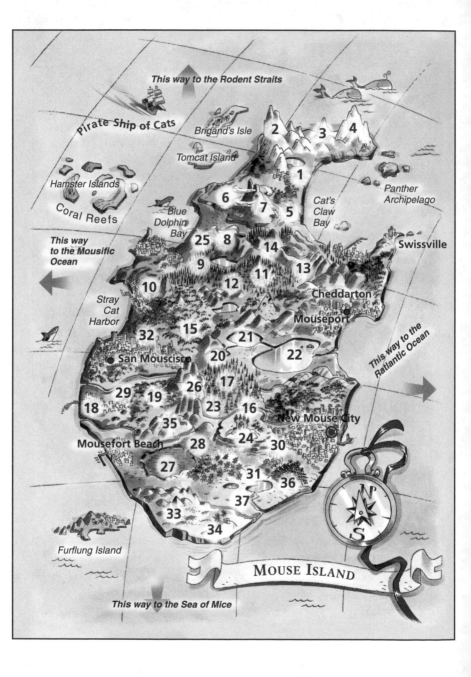

Map of Mouse Island

1. Big Ice Lake
2. Frozen Fur Peak
3. Slipperyslopes Glacier
4. Coldcreeps Peak
5. Ratzikistan
6. Transratania
7. Mount Vamp
8. Roastedrat Volcano
9. Brimstone Lake
10. Poopedcat Pass
11. Stinko Peak
12. Dark Forest
13. Vain Vampires Valley
14. Goose Bumps Gorge
15. The Shadow Line Pass
16. Penny Pincher Lodge
17. Nature Reserve Park
18. Las Ratayas Marinas
19. Fossil Forest
20. Lake Lake
21. Lake Lake Lake
22. Lake Lakelakelake
23. Cheddar Crag
24. Cannycat Castle
25. Valley of the Giant Sequoia
26. Cheddar Springs
27. Sulfurous Swamp
28. Old Reliable Geyser
29. Vole Vail
30. Ravingrat Ravine
31. Gnat Marshes
32. Munster Highlands
33. Mousehara Desert
34. Oasis of the Sweaty Camel
35. Cabbagehead Hill
36. Rattytrap Jungle
37. Rio Mosquito

Dear mouse friends,
Thanks for reading, and farewell
till the next book.
It'll be another whisker-licking-good
adventure, and that's a promise!

Geronimo Stilton